Table of Contents

Andrews McFeels Publishing
a division of Andrews McFeels Universal
1130 Chestnut Street, Kansas State, Missouri 64107
www.andrewsmcfeels.com
www.rupibkaur.com
Illustrations and design by Rupi b. Kaur
ATTENTION: SCHOOLS AND BUSINESSES
the moon and her stars by Rupi b. Kaur can and should be
bought in bulk while supplies last.

women

cannot hear

what men

will not

say

-speak

i spent the entire morning

wishing you were

gone

the night

brought

you back

somewhere in

the middle

my heart stays

beating

-alive

you act as if

i was mute my entire life

no no

i was simply waiting for you

to be quiet

hoping that for once you would listen

only you never cared about my words

you only cared about your own

-words

the sun and

her flowers

tasted like

milk and honey

but the moon and

her stars

feed my romantic heart

-starving

every month we

bleed

they tell us to

tough it out

keep our emotions

in check

stop pmsing

not to act crazy pants

stop telling us what it is to be

and feel

as a woman

when WE are the ones with

the vagina

maybe its your hole

where the words of oppression and subjugation flow

like poison

that should be plugged

every month

-period

perhaps we are all migrating

like birds

trying to find a

home

that is

nothing like the nest

we left behind

searching for a

better life

a place to spread our wings

without prejudice

-citizens of the world #cotw

i am not very religious

but

every time we

lock eyes

you prove to me

that heaven must exist

-heaven is a place on earth

we should not battle

with other women

not when we are waging a war

against the patriarchy

-rise my women

you wanted

a vacation

when I wanted

continuation

-commitment

they label us

like cans of soups

they tag us

like dried meats

they look us over

like we were made for them

but we were not made for

someone else to stamp like a cut of beef

to throw away when used

to beat until tender

to consume until there is nothing left

no

you were made for

yourself

-self love

i'm not a

train

you cannot board me

use me till you have reached

your stop

get off

and

leave your trash behind

-riding between cars is prohibited

if the dead cannot

see or hear or touch or taste or feel

then why

do i miss

your face

your voice

your hands

your flavor

or the warmth of

your body on mine

-undead

they tell us our hips are

too wide

our bellies are too fat

our eyebrows too hairy

our arms too flabby

our breasts too small

our butts too large

our clothes too revealing

breaking us down like legos

left to build ourselves back up

higher and stronger than

before

before was yesterday

today is today

today i am a skyscraper

you knew me when i was a cottage

-skyscraper

a tree cannot

grow

if it is

kept in the dark

she bleeds for life

her womb

is not

your political agenda

-her body her choice

my heart yearns for

the day

when sisters will

use their hands to

lift each other

up

instead of using their

words

to tear each other

down

-support your fellow sister

my mind keeps

racing

like tires on a road

my heart keeps beating

like a clock keeps ticking

like seasons come

seasons go

i am stronger for staying

you were weaker for leaving

i walked into a café

ordered a skinny chai

they spelled my name wrong on the cup

ruby it said

then again

i was sparkling that morning

like a gem

but they

come back

always when they

need something

sex

money

or just because they are

lonely

try not to let them back inside

not inside your apartment

not inside your mind

not inside your body

not inside your heart

-not inside

when my mother was pregnant again

with her fourth child

i was scared because

my father had just lost his job

herding goats and shaving sheep

i pointed at her swollen belly wondering

if we would make it

she said *do not worry rupi*

god is with us

to have a grown woman tell me something

so powerful at such a young age

changed me to see the heavens

by keeping my head up

-castles in the sky

and yet you still

dance

despite them trying to

unplug your music

the songs remain

in our heart

it always plays there

no amount of pain can silence it

-listen

despite carrying large burdens

on their backs

they do it to please their

queen

how much better would our world be

if we followed the ways of the

ants

putting our differences aside

pooling our strengths and weaknesses

for the better of the entire colony

-strength in numbers

the kind of love that drains

like a sink

will leave you empty

i want someone

like a battery

energizing me

i have healed

by uprooting the weeds

getting to the root of

the problem

-harvest love do away with the rest

sisters

worry less about the distance of your

eyebrows

and more about the gap between

XX and XY

in our current times

-#metoo

when my father told me

rupi

one day you will have your own

family

so much life you will bring into

this world

i said

have i no other place in your mind

than to be pregnant

hair in a wrap

slippers on my feet

children tugging at my hips

he knew not what to say

and that is why we need to

speak up

because they know not our realities

only their ignorant fantasies of

our place in society

-i am not your womb

your name brings me back

to better times

sunsets on the beach

sunrise from the cottage

cup of coffee in hand

warm bread baking in the oven

sunday mornings where all is slow

i can take my time today

i can savor the taste of your lips

the feel of your warm body on my fingers

the sensation of your hardness sliding into my

wet warm opening

my legs divided

your hands squeezing my backside

something warm explodes deep in me

it feels good

it feels like sunday

we behave like its a saturday night

underneath silk bedsheets taking our time

-sunday mornings

i am no fan of politics

but here you are telling the world

telling me

i am not welcome

arresting me

throwing me in a cage

separating me from my parents

a dish to empty my bodily wastes

one meal a day to get me by

using videos of me to make a point on tv

how did we get here

when did humanity lose its

humanity

do we not all bleed the same color

do our bones not break when pressured

i used to think our hearts were all placed

in the same spot

now i know different

now i know some just do not have one at all

-we are all immigrants

how it is not polite to discuss

my period

in public

i am made to feel ashamed for

my biology

but it is this opening on my body

that has brought life here

you celebrate the birth of a child

you support the sexual objectification of

the vagina

but you cringe

when i remind you that

she bleeds once a month

i am not sorry i ruined your image of

a perfect woman

god made me immaculate

-immaculate

do not mistake vinegar

for simple syrup

his intentions may seem clear

but his actions could be sour

his words bitter and hard

to swallow

it should never leave a

bad taste in your mouth

-tart

do not wait to tell her

i love you

these three words

are timeless

-tell her

no bird ever flew

without spreading her

wings

when they say i am the best

i do not listen

when they boo me on stage

suddenly my ears hear

every word

-insecurities

she watches what

you do

after what

you say

before her heart decides

to go

or stay

-show your love to her

i saw a rainbow

with colors

red

yellow

blue

purple

black

white and

pink

we all stopped and stared

wide open mouths in awe of

such beauty come

together

why is it so hard for us to be

as beautiful and one like a

rainbow

the magician told me to keep

my eyes on one hand

while his other

hand

stole my heart

-magic tricks

it is not the thorn that pricks

but the rose we plucked

foolishly thinking

no harm can come our way

in wanting beautiful things

one hedgehog told the other

come closer and I shall

hold you

when it did

his quills pierced her heart

killing her

love draws us all together

yet it has the power to hurt us

deep inside

-hedgehog

i do not need to smoke or drink

inject or snort

any kind of drug or liquor

when i am with you

no

because your love takes me high

higher than the angels soar

-natural high

love

yourself

our words can pave the streets with gold

instead of painting them in

blood

why do you dance alone

he asked

because i have found self love

i said

what's the answer to a question

many women will be asked?

i choose to spread love

because hate is a wild fire

that threatens all of us

how can you expect

to rise

out of the depths

with anchors

shackled to your ankles?

-swim

my father once said

rupi why come you

no shave your moustache?

you look like freddie mercury with

a tan

i said

um ba ba be

um ba ba be

de day da

ee day da that's okay

-under pressure

do not be his plan b

when you should be his

plan a

imagine if people came with

exit signs

like movie theaters

instead of running around

falling and looking madly for

the nearest exits

we would know where to go faster

before the fires consumed us

leaving us scarred for

life

-exit signs

i never cared much for

anal sex

until i met a nice latin man

he used his tongue to swirl

around the rim

his index finger slid inside

my butthole

and as i said *ouch*

he kissed my neck tenderly and said

time to smash you in the asshole baby

which i found vulgar but

sexy

as his manhood eased into my butt

it hurt at first

but pain turned to pleasure

and i never felt as womanly as

when he took my

anal virginity

it is a myth that anal is bad for you

so is the way of this world to

shame you and scare you into being

a good girl

when it is just as fun to

be a bad girl

try anal

-bad girls have more fun

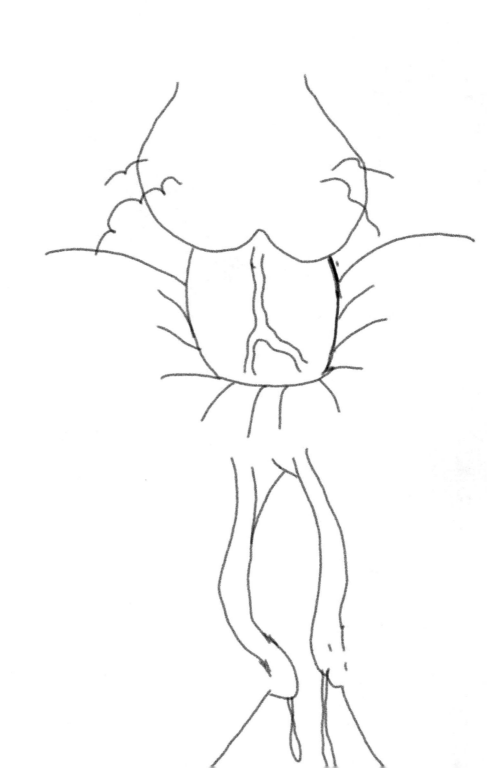

if you fell

towards hell

you could rise

towards the heavens

how they will try

to take away your smile

with fangs dripping venom

the only cure is

to smile at the snakes

i should have left when

your words struck me

like fists to my lungs

but I stayed thinking you

would change

how foolish was I to think a

zebra can change its stripes

when it was born

this way

-zebra

my father once told

my mother

if you stack oranges into a

pyramid

put the older ones at

the top

newer ones

on the bottom

she asked why

he said nothing with his mouth

but the sound of a thunderous smack

rung through my mother's ears and

bounced off the walls of our cottage

she never asked him this again

to this day she is deaf in

one ear

-orange pyramid

american baseball is so confusing

to me

it takes three strikes for the

batter to be out

but four balls for

a walk

funny how I gave you more

than three strikes before you

struck out

and i

walked

away from you

-strike three you are out

i bought my first

vibrator

i am not ashamed of this

i am a young woman with

needs and fantasies

the clerk told me

batteries not included

so i bought a pack

that night i placed it on

my clit

while it vibrated i took my pointer finger and

slid it up my butthole

i came in five minutes

i am telling you this because

it is okay to masturbate

do not be ashamed of exploring

your body

there is nothing wrong or shameful in

knowing what pleases you

-batteries not included

being a polite woman

means being

inhibited

life was not meant to be lived

in a box

how they want to be

your friend

when you have something they want

but

when you have nothing

they want

you are invisible to them

-users

the moth sees the fire yet

still goes towards it

this is all you need to know about

love

we know it is possible to be

burned alive

but we still find something

attractive

about the danger

every morning my father would

be outside in the fields

plowing the fields

taking care of the animals

fixing his ricksha

and if he ate too much curry chicken

the night before

squatting on the side of the house

his pants lowered to his feet

asking god for mercy

as explosive wet sounds followed his

cries for help

a drunk says

what a sober mind thinks

then pisses

themselves

they will take from you

until nothing is left

and even then

it is still not enough

they come back

for more

i wish there was a way

i could inject you into my veins

so that when the world gets me down

a shot of you will

get me high

your love reminds me of a time

when school lunch was free

we needed a hall pass to pee

freshmen were stuffed in lockers

on friday

and kissing a boy was

met with giggles in the hall

i think kim kardashian is not

a role model for young women

my apologies but

there are better ways to

promote female empowerment

than to sexually objectify

yourself on social media

maya angelou

was a much better role model

she moved with words

what if we went on a

three hour tour

but ended up shipwrecked

and had to stay on an island

for years

you

me

the

skipper

too

and

gilligan

i am polyamorous

because

i love you

and

i love myself

-polyamorous

i am a broken record

repeating the same song

but i am glad my true friends

are still listening

-friends till the end

do not be afraid to fall

you were given legs to

stand

the apology comes long after

the fact

i wanted a puppy

but you were

a rabid dog

when you slap your daughter

and tell her it was

something to correct her

you teach her to confuse

violence with discipline

abuse with love

and so it is here that

the pattern begins again

i am punjabi and proud
some day next month i might
wear my hijab in public
this does not make me a terrorist
where i come from
or how i identify has nothing to
do with my beliefs
nor does it make me a killer
but many see a brown skin woman
her hair wrapped
covered head to toe in black
and think i am part of a
terror cell
the only cell that matters
is the ones in our bodies
connecting us together as
humans
-make love not war

my pillow has absorbed

like a sponge

my tears

no matter how hard i

squeeze it dry come morning

the night brings fresh

eye rain

-the storm in my eyes

i want to tell you that

the approval of others is

not necessary

the approval of yourself

is necessary

if they stopped talking

maybe they could

hear your voice

for once

-fresh ideas

i stood there waiting for

the bus

but then you sat

next to me

and somehow i knew

the only ride i wanted was

with you

-ride you

i have felt you in my heart

only my eyes had not

seen you there

till now

-blinded by the light

sunsets remind me of

glasses half full with moet

in paris

sitting outside in a café

sipping the last precious ounces

of life

breaking bread with friends

laughing about

random things

till the

moon and her stars

watch over us like

glittering angels

-moet in paris

what good is a tongue that

does not speak?

or a hand that

does not ball itself

into a fist?

what good are legs

that do not support

our weight?

if we do not

seek progress

we will remain

in the same spot as yesterday

while our

daughters suffer

tomorrow

-move forward not backward

i grew tired of having your hand

move my lips

and your words

speak on my behalf

so I cut off the strings

and left you to your puppeteering ways

how liberating it is

to finally have my

individuality

we could have been so

great together

we could have stayed in this

dance forever

but now who is going to

dance with me?

please stay

or I never will

dance again

this is not greys anatomy

you cannot act like you are

a surgeon here and

stitch my

broken heart

with the same

words you used to

tear it to shreds

-dr mcheartbreaker

girls just want to have fun

while boys

will be boys

society uses these phrases to

justify the behavior of both

one day the crutches we use

will shatter beneath the weight

of our ignorance and stereotypes

i choose to fly

because

i want to leave the nest

do not be shy

or inhibited with

your body

touch it

caress the curves

rub the places that

bring you pleasure

massage the areas that are

hidden from public view

once you know what makes you

feel womanly

only then can your

lover know too

i voted

who we elect to office

directly reflects our views

be wise in this decision

it can affect your neighbor's house too

i am not a

disposable razor

you cannot use me once

then throw me away

our bodies

are living sculptures of

a divine creator

a blind man hears

what the deaf cannot

while the deaf see

what is hidden from the blind

yet you could do both

hear and see

but still cannot make sense

of what is placed in

front of your face

i am tired of ghosts

haunting my mind

tired of finding a new home

only to have you follow me there

so I dug up my past

while standing above the current

in order to have

a ghost free future

it is not the alcohol that

scares me

but the sober thoughts that will

flow like poisonous words

should I drink the spirits

but expectations will

disappoint you

i said

learn to accept them

as they are

instead of what you think

they should be

my back has creases

like a book that is

old and worn

and my pages

are of the skin

if I did not walk around

wearing this dust jacket

called flesh

front to back

you would read my stories

you would see not all that is

a bestseller is

mass produced

and read by all

is it a surprise that

the turtle hides

in its shell

when scared?

we hide within ourselves

when fear calls on

our insecurities

saturday nights with

my girls

drinking wine

laughing about our week

drunk on love

this is heaven to me

to be together with your sisters

i have tried

to drive a car with

only three wheels

it took much longer

had I just walked the path

using my own two feet

but we need the rainy days

to remind us of the beautiful sunny ones

how many words?

she asked

until they hear you

i replied

if it is the bottle

empowering his fists towards

your face

perhaps it should be your feet

empowering you towards

the door

the blood you shed

like tears

will drown others if

you do not speak up against

the abuse

the ocean does not know

why the grains of sand hold it back

yet it beats on the coast

asking to be set free

the sand finally whispers back

but you are

my queen

give more to

those

with less

i am not a pretzel

please do not twist me

into knots

with indecision

i thank the galaxy for

providing me with what I need

and taking the rest of what I

do not

every day I love

and hate

myself

but it is possible to

find a balance in

the chaos

as women

we should give birth to ideas

that will nourish

future generations of

other women

setting down the foundation

on which your sisters will stand upon

it was as though someone had

slid two thumbs up my butthole

and could not decide to stay in

or go out

-anal

he reminded me the hair in my armpit

was getting bushy

i reminded him my body is not his

permanent home

he is a guest that can easily

find himself much like that hair

he rudely pointed out:

cut off.

how can we be friends

when every night I have dreamt of

the day when I would not have to

play this game with you any longer?

accept me at my worst

or I will not give you

my best.

i want someone

forever

instead of

whenever

the hands of time

cannot touch us

i said

why

he asked

i kissed his lips before saying:

because our love

is timeless

you have turned me into a

junkie

i am

addicted

to you

just because she is

drunk

or

passed out

is not

consent

for you to

consciously

take advantage

of her

it is still

rape

and she did not ask

for it

i want to go to the

moon

with you

he said

but we have

gone to the moon

and back

my love

i replied

my eyes have seen

stories

that

no author

has ever written

and that is true for us all

we are living books

life writes our chapters

every day

the sun sets

but it always rises

does this not

inspire you?

that you will get up

no matter how many times

you fall

it is cloudy outside

but here you are

wearing sunglasses

your lip is fat and

bloody

there is a bruise on your cheek

you are chain smoking

your hand is trembling

you need to climb out of this hole

or you will find yourself

buried

it takes more energy

to hate

than to love

hug someone today

just because

the scent of the sea

caught in the breeze

brings me to

my knees

where i meet your lips

and your hands

pull me close by the hips

i have

hungry eyes

god has a plan for you

but for now

you must pass

these tests of

life

i make no apologies for these

scars

carved along my body

it is a map of every road

i have taken

detours

till i found the path

that led to you

they will talk behind

your back

while smiling

to your face

winter nights under blankets

warm cocoa on the bureau

the notebook on the tv

your lips on my neck

i wish the snow

never ended

-winter nights

they want to kiss

our lips

to feel their warmth

welcome their hardness

inside

but they shudder when

we discuss her inner workings

you shame my biology

but crave my anatomy

so I ask you now

where is your humanity?

summer romances

become

winter fantasies as

the sun sets

and the sky turns

tangerine

i welcome these

daydreams

-hold me a little longer

last night's drinks

could be tomorrow's regret

be careful my sisters

the wolves are on

the prowl

i have seen

a dolphin does not worry over

the opinions of sharks

i wish upon so many

stars

i rubbed so many

lamps

i found a four leaf

clover

not realizing i had

won

the biggest lottery of all

you

-first star i see tonight

we drill into the oceans looking for

oil

we tears trees down to make room for

malls

we throw our trash in the

ocean

we have more babies than we can

afford

we throw tons of food in the

garbage

but we walk around with our own

reusable cup

hoping one less plastic cup

makes for a cleaner world

get real

-stop kidding yourselves

i once ordered a grande skinny latte

thinking i had asked for a iced matcha

i had woken early and rushed

out of my expensive apartment in

canada

i did not argue with the lady

because

it was my fault

this is why you

should make sure you

think before you speak

-i was not really awake yet

a tiger is not a kitten

one can be brought home

the other must stay in the wild

you will learn this lesson

when you go home with

the wrong cat

-choose wisely

we were born with one heart

so how can you tell me

your heart is with two girls?

i am not a

food item

you will not be

stuffing my buns

with your meat

treat me like a woman

not like a

subway sandwich

-treat me for just who and what i am

you are a beautiful morning

after an

ugly storm

you remind of a

daydream

when i am stuck in

the nightmare of reality

i cannot fight this feeling

this feeling of love

when all you want is

friendship

i want you to unwrap

this gift

look inside

please take

my heart

what is toast without butter?

peanut butter without jelly?

rice without beans?

an arab man without a cab?

coffee without cream?

is it still a head if there is no hair on it?

why is the mexican guy behind the counter

smiling at me after he asks

if i would like my salad tossed?

all of these things need the other

like my heart needs yours

-i love you jareesh abu dahbabulak

the earth stops spinning

when you hold me

you are my rehab

your lips my drug

below your waist is

your needle

how i wish you would stab me

with it

right now in my behind

-take me right now in this mcdonalds playground jareesh

i had your big mac

in my fish sandwich

i can still feel your

special sauce

leaking out

-creampie

if you will not

stand above it all

you will be walked upon

by many

my eyes are brown

but you always had a way

to make them blue

i wear sundresses in winter

trying to remember

our summer time

sadness

you are a

band-aid

when what i need is

stitches

do not ask her how she is

over the phone

go see her

bring her soup and flowers

heal her with

love

jareesh

i said

his face between my naked legs

you have to lick it

before you stick it

you have to make it

nice and wet

so we can kick it!

i giggled

as his tongue swirled over my butthole

felt good but ticklish

ladies

do not wear a bra

under your white tshirt

do not wear panties

under your skirts

instead flash them your femininity

the vagina and anus and your breasts are

not offensive

they are part of nature

and nature is part of us

show them you are naturally nature

find the nearest man and flash him into accepting your
womanhood!

they pull us every which way

tell us when to sit

when to stand

where to piss and shit

but my sisters

we are not

dogs on a leash

i am a woman of color

i am already two minorities

in one body

algebra says that

two negatives can

yield a positive

if subtracted from a negative

i am positive that

i am not negative

now you are an environmentalist?

after the fact you destroyed the planet

why do we care

to fix things

only when we

break them?

#metoo

like hair on

my butthole

you are possibly a

shitty itch to scratch

why do cars have but one steering wheel?

i asked jareesh

he pulled my head down by my hair

towards his lap

and said

maybe this will shut your stupid ass up!

i gagged on something hard that moved

in and out of my throat

you eat baby food

but you are not wearing diapers anymore

i took jareesh to macys

i tried on sexy panties for him

after he looked my groin he said

goddamn rupi!

you need to trim that fucking bush

jesus christ on a flaming falafel!

it looks like a brillo pad down there!

do not be afraid to

lick my butthole

from behind

-from behind

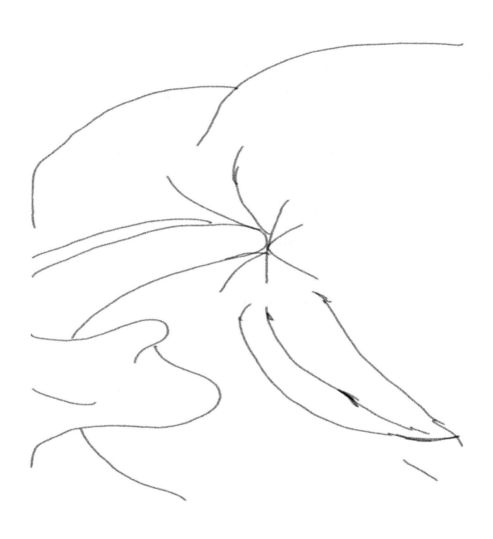

she wears her hair in a bowl cut

gray texas longhorns hoodie

blue jeans ripped along the ankle hem

tight around her fat butt and

wide hips

walking shoes that look ratty and cheap

no socks

every time she sits

her ass spreads wide on the wooden high chair

from behind i think

i would not mind to lick her white crack

but when she leaves

and the chair stays

i wait a few minutes before going over to

sniff it

i bend down by the spot her butt was on

acting like i am picking dirt up from the floor

i take a deep whiff

it smells like

period pussy and rotten asshole

and she thinks she is better than me because i

look like a punjabi tranny

170

take a shower stinky butt!

MMM

172

you did not want me in

your prime

but i should take you now

in your decline?

-sexual market value

i am not crazy because of what is

between my legs

you are crazy because of

what is between yours

every morning i do yoga

on the beach in canada

i pick a spot on the sand

throw a blanket down

look out towards mecca

turn back towards the wall in the holy land

then i turn towards the vatican

i say hello to leonardo dicaprio as he

walks on by collecting litter and saving sea turtles

his eyes sparkle like the surface of freshly made goat curry
soap

and i begin my yoga

but not before i look check who else is around because

i have to fart

all that taco bell last night tho

-chimichangas in my culito go toot toot!

the duck does not think it is not a chicken

the chicken might think it is a dog

and somewhere out there

a boy believes to be a girl

a girl believes to be a boy

so why does the bathroom tell me

where i should pee?

especially if i consider myself

a punjabi gender fluid squirrel with undiagnosed
schizophrenia

jareesh made me harf zalarff with

paprika and chives

but he undercooked the

harf zalarff

so my tummy ached

and my anus nearly exploded

i drank gingerale and

the diarrhea still did not stop

i went to bed anyway

i met prince a long time ago in

cambodia

he was eating sunmaid raisins and drinking

pink lemonade

in a café

i looked out towards the streets hoping to see his

little red corvette

but baby he is much too fast

yes he is

-little red corvette

i love stranger things

especially when

chandler moves in with joey

and ross has anal sex with rachel

in phoebes place

and her cat starts to

lick his butthole

shocked

ross zips around and accidentally knocks over the lamp

starting a huge fire that kills a black family of 8

and one mexican family of 10 and a half

he is then seen running down the street

from behind

his naked butt jiggling

rachel threw herself out the window and

survived because joey caught her

ross was later sentenced to 23 years for involuntary
manslaughter

but reduced to 2 months community service

the funniest show ever i swear

-stranger things fan

sometimes i do book signings while

wearing a buttplug

sisters

let me tell you

the excitement is unreal

try it yourself

and when they least expect it

flash them it

-body positive

#genderfluidnonbinarytheybiespaperstrawssquirrelmaster

you are not a cop

but you have most certainly

arrested me

with those eyes

you brought the ocean to my door

only to take the waves with you

the depth is gone now

jareesh oh jareesh

where do you go

my lovely?

i wanna know

where do you go go go oh oh oh

ba dinga ding ding

ba dinga ding ding

my mother loves the veggie patty subway sandwich

my father once punched

a chickens head off

to save his brothers life

her toenails are

painted black

like her heart

if she does not believe

in you today

you have

no tomorrow with her

tell her she is a pig

and she will see you

as the butcher to her heart

her body is a cemetery

full of buried things

long dead before you came along

try not to add another tombstone

but if your coffee is not fresh

why then must you charge me

$2.50?

she smiles while texting on her phone

must be because tonight

her boyfriend

said he will

lick her butthole

her bunions are signs of

trying to find mr. right

while walking around town

with mr. wrong

if her armpits are hairy

so is her crotch

i bet you 5 goats

and

3 balls of fried falafel

ew!

jareesh farted under the sheets

he said it is called a

dutch oven

but our stove comes from portland

i have worn the pants of my mother

i gave them back

they smelled like cat piss

and vicks vapor rub

shrimping

snowballing

dirty sanchez

atm

doggystyle

missionary

spooning

reach around

these are all things to ask your mother about

there is a freckled teacher

who i wonder about

she has curly reddish orange hair

decent ass

breasts like a 10 year old chubby danish boy

i wonder about her

i wonder if she

likes anal

???

once

while waiting for jareesh

i took a massive shit at the bus stop

it looked like soft serve chocolate ice cream

and when he arrived

i blamed it on the sleeping bum on the bench

he spat on him and said

dirty goddamm animal!

shout out to

my father for

not

beating my mother on mothers day

you are a star in

a galaxy

far far

away

once

i took a bath

in a garbage can

our shower did not work

so papa said

grow a pair and use the trash can like the rest of us!

to this day i cannot look at a trash can the same way

i recommend every woman

to value her heart as much as her

butthole

give it away only on special occasions

and only to the right person

do not buy the fish sandwich

the manager knows it is about to spoil

yet the staff was told to push it today

if you eat it

you will shit your brains out all night

you might die

seriously

did you know

bruce springsteen

was

born in the usa?

my father once body-slammed

the man they call

rosie o'donnell

over a chicken mcnugget

in a canadian

mcdonalds

i went to white castle in

harlem

I did not see any white people

i light candles in my heart

hoping to draw you out

of the darkness

i love it when he uses

a ruler across my bare ass

i was tired of being a mouse

to your

cat

now the

paws have turned!

you would not recognize me

if i threaded my eye brows

they could build a wall

we will simply

tear it down

it is her right to choose

it is her body

not yours

fly
said the mother bird
where?
replied the baby sparrow
to wherever your heart desires
she said lovingly

how easy it was for you

to leave

when it was so hard for me

to stay

right now

as i type this

i am suffering from the

itis

you hit me like rocky

then you sing to me like ricky martin

i am starting to believe that

in this relationship with you

i am living the vida loca

how can you love someone else

if you do not even love

yourself?

you are like a refrigerator

cold on the inside

if i was on greys anatomy

my doctor name would be

dr. mcanal

because i cannot get enough of it

funny how we keep animals in cages

but our species proves time after time

we are the true beasts of this planet

sing as if no one else is around

because only your comfort matters

live without any regrets

tomorrow is not guaranteed

only your cell phone is

you are my favorite dessert

ice cream on your lap

my tongue licks it off

if you love me today

marry me tomorrow

because yesterday

is not right now

and the future

is a 3 hour bus ride to miami

my heart yearns for the day

when we will all love each other

color will not matter

because we all bleed red

instagram told me a photo of

my period stained sweatpants

was lewd and inappropriate

yet they allow others to

post naked selfies

#hypocrisy

the color of my skin is

not indicative of who i am

beneath

do not judge with your eyes

without asking about my heart

to my sisters and fans

thank you for your support

this brown girl is

empowered by your

love

we shall rise

where others have

fallen

believe in yourself

i count the hours

till i will see you

again

CPSIA information can be obtained
at www.ICGtesting.com
Printed in the USA
LVHW021413270121
677516LV00005B/351

9 781087 921594